# THIS IGLOO BOOK BELONGS TO:

.................................................................

igloobooks

*Published in 2019*
*by Igloo Books Ltd*
*Cottage Farm*
*Sywell*
*NN6 0BJ*
*www.igloobooks.com*

1019 001
2 4 6 8 10 9 7 5 3 1
ISBN 978-1-83852-223-0

*The Yeti Who Came to Stay: written by Melanie Joyce and illustrated by Katya Longhi*
*What's That Noise?: written by Stephanie Moss and illustrated by Mark Jones*
*When I Grow Up: written by Melanie Joyce and illustrated by Lizzie Walkley*
*Who's Afraid of the Dark?: written by Melanie Joyce and illustrated by David Creighton-Pester*

*Designed by Alex Alexandrou*
*Edited by Hannah Cather*

*Printed and manufactured in China*

# BIG STORIES
## FOR LITTLE
# HEROES

igloobooks

Once, Billy read a story that was exciting and a little bit scary, about a creature called a yeti, who was **smelly, tall** and **hairy.**

No one had ever seen it. They said it could **never** be found, because all it left behind were footprints on the ground.

"Can we search for the yeti?" Billy begged his dad one day.

I bet that we could find him and bring him back here to stay.

"Oh, **alright**," said Dad, with a sigh. "If you **really** insist.
But I have to tell you honestly, I don't think yetis exist."

Billy packed his backpack
and set off with his dad.

"Have fun," said his mum, waving,
thinking their plan quite mad.

They sailed across the sea,
took a train and rode on a bus.

**Ding! Ding!** went the bell.
Dad said, "This is the stop for us."

At the top of a mountain, they found footprints in the snow.

"Follow me," Billy said to Dad.

"I know which way to go."

At last, they found the yeti. He was huge and covered in fur. "What's **your** name?" asked Billy. The yeti answered,

"urgh!"

"Urgh!" replied the yeti, smiling.
Billy took that as a 'yes'.

But what the yeti really said was anybody's guess.

Back home, Mum was shocked and said,

Oh dear, goodness me. I hadn't really thought about what a yeti might eat for tea!

14

The yeti ate pretty much everything, even Brussels sprouts and peas.

He didn't use a knife and fork, or say 'excuse me,' 'thank you,' or 'please.'

15

Billy didn't mind that his new friend **slobbered** and **slurped**, or that he snored at night, smelled awful and often **burped**...

... because the yeti was so much fun.
He just wanted to play.

He didn't really understand why
people kept running away.

17

The days passed by so happily
and the two friends played together.

They loved to go exploring...

... and stayed out in all weather.

The yeti chased after Billy and bounced on the trampoline.

"**Whoo-hoo!**" shouted Billy, giggling.

It was the **highest** he'd ever been.

19

The yeti smiled all the time, until one night it began to snow.

"He's missing his home," said Mum.
"It's time for him to go."

So, the yeti went back home. Billy felt lonely every day.
He really missed his friend and wished he hadn't gone away.

Then, one morning in the mail,
a postcard dropped on the mat.

'Urgh!' was all it said
and only a yeti would write that.

urgh!

So Billy packed his suitcase and went to visit his best friend.
And he was very sure, their friendship would never end.

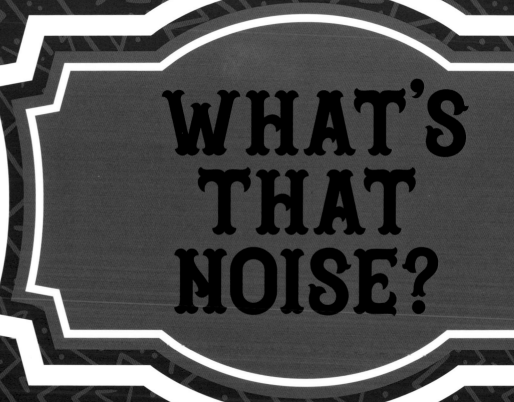

One dark, summer's night, there was
a strange, low, rumbling sort of a roar.

It grew louder and louder and louder...
and then it rumbled again some more.

WHAT'S THAT NOISE?

cried Baby Bunny,
feeling nothing but dread and fright.

Though what crossed Baby Badger's face
was a look of curious delight.

Finally, Baby Badger said,

Come on, Bunny, that's enough!
It's no good imagining all this
silly, crazy
stuff.

36

As an orchestra

# CROAKED,

one frog stopped to say...

... "I wish that **rumbling** would stop. It's been **roaring** all day!"

So they continued their search, looking this way and that,

until they stumbled on Fox, hitting acorns with a bat!

Suddenly, the real
**rumbling**
noise was clearer than ever,

so Baby Badger and Baby Bunny
both huddled close together.

40

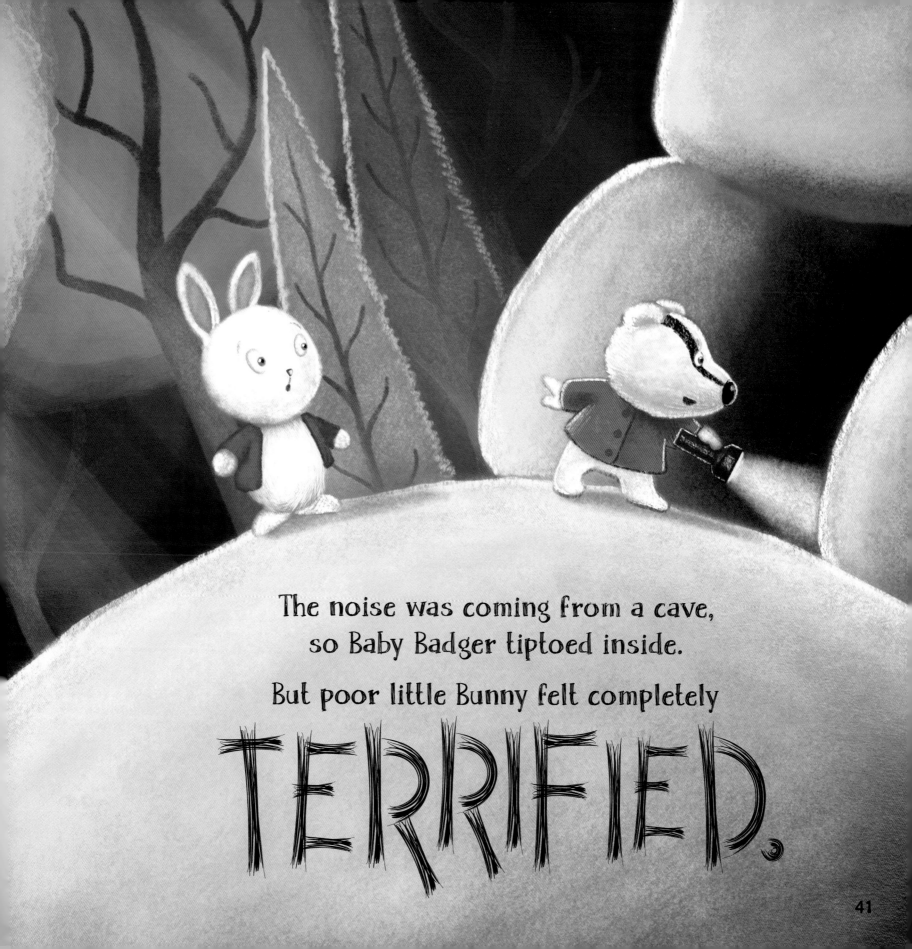

The noise was coming from a cave,
so Baby Badger tiptoed inside.

But poor little Bunny felt completely

TERRIFIED.

Bunny hid behind Badger,
in case they came to any harm.

But when they peered inside,
she saw there was no
cause for alarm.

Baby Bunny said,

It's
Big Bear!
The noise was
him all along.

"A bit of snoring isn't scary.

How could I have been so wrong?"

So they **banged** on pots and pans.

They even **bounced** up on the bed.

It took a while, but Big Bear soon woke up and rubbed his head.

YAWN, YAWN, STRETCH, went Big Bear.
The sound made all the cave walls shake.
I can't believe I overslept. What a terrible mistake!

Before everybody knew it,
a forest party was in full swing.

And Baby Bunny learned facing
your fears is more important
than anything.

WHEN I
GROW UP

When I grow up, I'll be **famous**.
I'll be a mega star.

I'll wear a sparkly silver costume
and play an electric **guitar**.

When I grow up, I'll be **royal.**
Maybe I'll get to be Queen.

I'll have more crowns and tiaras than anyone's **ever** seen.

I'll be an **inventor** when I grow up.
What I make will be a surprise.

Everyone will be so **amazed,**
they won't believe their eyes.

I'll be a **pirate** when I grow up.
I'll join a pirate crew.

58

We'll look for clues on our special map
and dig up **treasure**, too.

I'll be a **magician** when I grow up.
I'll pull rabbits out of a hat.

When I grow up, I'll be an **astronaut.**
I'll fly a rocket up to Mars.

I'll **whizz** around the moon,
and bring back lots of stars.

I'll be a **ballerina** when I grow up,
with a tutu and pink ballet shoes.

I'll leap across the stage,
and get lots of **"Aahs!"** and **"Oohs!"**

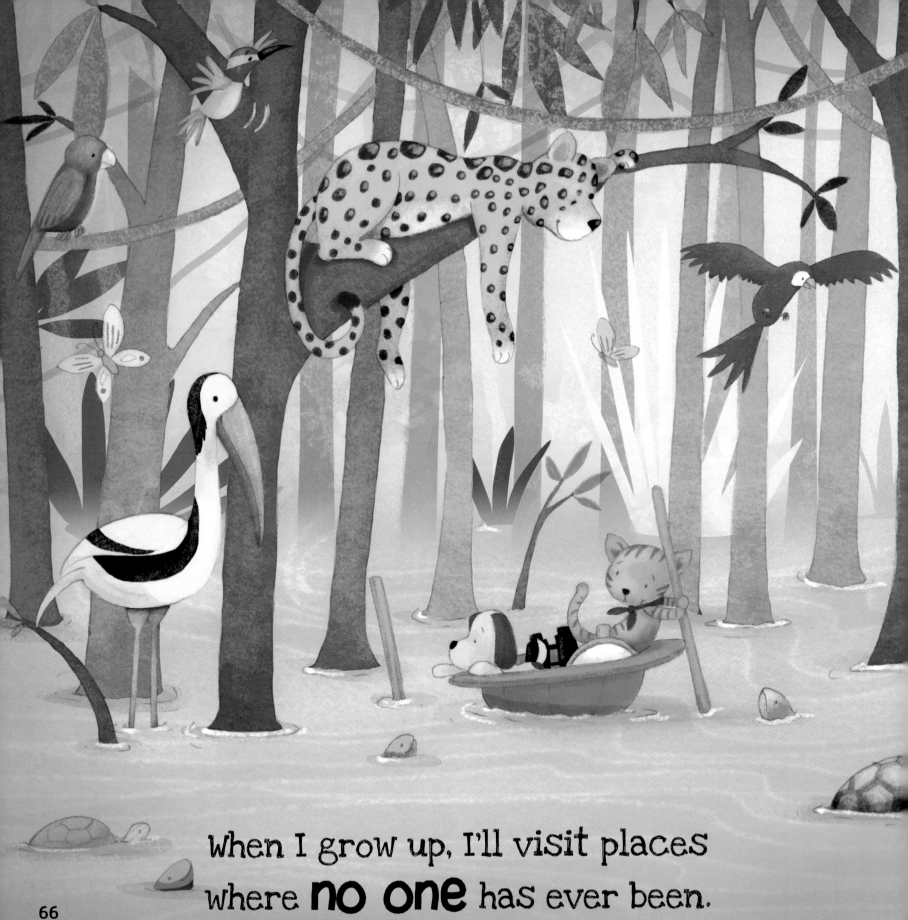

When I grow up, I'll visit places
where **no one** has ever been.

When I come back, I'll tell stories about the **amazing** things I've seen.

I'll be an **explorer** when I grow up, with an enormous magnifying glass.

68

I'll search for strange new creatures that might be **lurking** in the grass.

69

I'm sure that when I grow up,
there will be **lots** of things I can be.

But I won't think about that right now,
because we've got spaghetti for tea.

71

If you go into the dark
and tiptoe about at night,
nothing will look the same
as it does when it is light.

The sun will sink from the sky
and the moon will shine fat and round.

Shapes will creep from the wood and STRETCH along the ground.

But there's no need to worry
or for you to be afraid.
The shapes are only shadows
that the branches of trees have made.
It's true, the dark is full of things that
CREAK and CRACK and MOAN.

Things that JUMP,
things that go BUMP
and things that
GRUMBLE and GROAN.

79

But you'll find it's just a badger, MUNCHING on a midnight snack,

SHUFFLING over twigs and sticks along the forest track.

Perhaps he'll stop for a chat
or play a game or two.
Then he'll be on his way,
wave goodbye and say,
"THANK YOU!"

If you do go into the dark,

always remember to look behind,

because lurking in the shadows,

who knows what you might find?

Bats could fly out of the trees

and get tangled in your hair,

or suddenly you'll hear a

SNAP and ask...

It will only be the night owl
SWOOPING through the sky.
HOO-HOO! he'll say to you,
as he goes flying by.

The fluffy owlets in the nest might sing a song for you.
They'll flap their wings and go, TE-WIT, TE-WIT, TE-WOO! 85

But are there really monsters hiding in places you can't see?

And do you think to yourself,

"ARE THEY FOLLOWING ME?"

Don't worry, it's only the hedgehogs, SHUFFLING by the wall,
making their way back to their house, and not monsters after all.

87

If you go out into the dark
and miss the daytime sun...

... remember that playing in the
moonlight can really be lots of fun.

You can SPLASH in glittery pools
and watch the little fish.
If a shooting star ZOOMS by,
then you can make a magic wish.

When you hear a
**SCRITCH** and **SCRATCH**
or maybe a distant **HOWL,**
it will only be a guard dog
or maybe a kitty on the prowl.

You will hear noises at night
and wonder what they could be.
It doesn't mean they're scary,
just because you can't see.

91

So if you're afraid of the dark
and think you should beware,
remember that you're not alone and
someone will always be there.

You'll get a hug and a kiss,

and maybe a story, too.

Then you'll yawn and know that

it really is bedtime for you.

You'll just curl up, safe and warm, in the glow of the light.

And think of all the things
that you saw in the night.
You might hear a SNAP,
a HOOT, a CRACK or a BARK,
but you'll know just what it is
and won't be afraid of the dark.